THIS BOOK BELONGS TO

_____

PEANUTS®
It's the Easter Beagle,
CHARLIE BROWN

By Charles M. Schulz
Based on the animated special, the text was adapted by Daphne Pendergrass
Illustrated by Vicki Scott

Simon Spotlight
New York   London   Toronto   Sydney   New Delhi

SIMON SPOTLIGHT
An imprint of Simon & Schuster Children's Publishing Division
1230 Avenue of the Americas, New York, New York 10020
This Simon Spotlight edition January 2016
SIMON SPOTLIGHT and colophon are registered trademarks of Simon & Schuster, Inc. For information about special discounts for bulk purchases, please contact Simon & Schuster Special Sales at 1-866-506-1949 or business@simonandschuster.com. Manufactured in China 1015 LEO
10 9 8 7 6 5 4 3 2 1 ISBN 978-1-4814-6159-7   ISBN 978-1-4814-6160-3 (eBook)

The winter snow has melted, the birds are tweet-tweet-tweeting in the trees, and all the flowers are in bloom—it's Easter time, and the whole neighborhood is getting ready!

Marcie is on her way to Peppermint Patty's house to decorate Easter eggs. Marcie has never decorated Easter eggs before.

"I got the eggs, sir, just like you asked," Marcie says when Peppermint Patty opens the door.

"Great! Come on in," Peppermint Patty says. "But quit calling me 'sir'!"

In the kitchen, Peppermint Patty hops up on a stool and starts mixing the dyes. "You get the eggs ready," she tells Marcie.

Marcie isn't sure what to do, so she heads over to the stove, cracks each egg, and puts them on the skillet one by one.

"Uh, sir," Marcie says after a while. "How do we color the eggs after we fry them?"

Peppermint Patty stares at the broken shells in disbelief. *"AAUGH!"* she cries.

Across the neighborhood, Lucy leans on Schroeder's piano while he plays an airy spring song.

"We've got another one of those great holidays coming up," Lucy hints while he plays. "Where boys have the opportunity to give presents to pretty girls."

Schroeder stops playing and rolls his eyes. "It's not a time for *getting,*" he scoffs. "It's a time of renewal—the start of spring."

"Wrong," Lucy says with a grin. "It's the gift-getting season."

At Charlie Brown's house, his little sister, Sally, is looking at her worn-out old shoes. "It's almost Easter, and I have nothing to wear!" Sally cries.

Linus and Lucy come by on their way to the store. "We need Easter baskets, eggs, candy—the works. Want to join us?" Lucy offers.

"I told you it's a waste of time," Linus says. "The Easter Beagle does all that."

"Linus, you drive me crazy!" Lucy shouts at her little brother.

"Who's the Easter Beagle?" Sally asks.

"On Easter Sunday, the Easter Beagle passes colored eggs to all the good little kids," Linus explains.

But Sally isn't so sure she believes him—she remembers waiting with Linus for the Great Pumpkin on Halloween. She stayed up all night, and the Great Pumpkin never came!

"Come on, Sally," Charlie Brown says. "I thought you wanted to get some new shoes."

At the store, Charlie Brown, Sally, Snoopy, Linus, and Lucy run into Peppermint Patty and Marcie. "We're here to get some eggs to color for Easter!" Peppermint Patty says. "Marcie here fried the last batch."

"It's a waste of time to buy and color eggs," Linus says again. "The Easter Beagle will do all that."

Peppermint Patty looks from Linus to Charlie Brown. "Easter Beagle? Boy, Chuck, you sure have some strange friends. Come on. Let's go in and buy some eggs!"

While Snoopy is looking around, he comes across a display of big hollow Easter eggs. He picks one up and looks inside—there's a picture of bunnies dancing!

Snoopy imagines that he's celebrating Easter with the bunnies too. Snoopy loves doing his happy dance with his new bunny friends.

After Sally buys her new pair of shoes, Marcie and Peppermint Patty get their eggs, and Lucy stocks up on Easter supplies, the gang decides to head home.

But all the way back, Linus still tries to convince everyone to believe in the Easter Beagle.

Lucy finally loses her patience. "Good grief!" she cries. "There is *no* Easter Beagle!"

When they get home, Peppermint Patty starts making a new set of dyes for the Easter eggs. This time Marcie is sure she'll get it right, but just in case, she puts some eggs in the waffle iron, two in the toaster, and the rest in the oven! *"AAUGH!"* Peppermint Patty yells everytime she sees Marcie ruin another batch.

With all the eggs ruined again, Marcie and Peppermint Patty start the long journey back to the store.

"You're making a mistake!" Linus cries as they walk by. "The Easter Beagle will take care of it all."

"Really? Sir, is this right?" Marcie asks.

Peppermint Patty turns to Linus. "Look, I'm having enough trouble without all of your fantastic stories," she says. "Come on, Marcie!"

A few hours later with fresh eggs in hand, Peppermint Patty goes over the plan once more. "These eggs are not to be fried, roasted, toasted, or waffled. These eggs must be *boiled*."

So Marcie fills up a big pot with water and turns on the stove. Then she cracks each egg and adds it to the pot!

After a while, Marcie calls over to Peppermint Patty, "The eggs look done, sir."

Peppermint Patty hops off her stool. "That's funny," she says, sniffing the air. "It smells like soup."

When Peppermint Patty gets over to the stove, she finds out why. "Marcie!" she cries. "You made egg soup! *AAUGH!*"

With the last of the eggs gone, and no money to buy more, it seems like this Easter is shaping up to be a disaster. "Chuck, I just don't know what to do. How am I supposed to teach Marcie about Easter and coloring eggs?" Peppermint Patty asks.

"Don't worry. The Easter Beagle will come and bring eggs to all the little kids," Linus reminds the gang.

"I hope you're right," Peppermint Patty says, sighing.

But Lucy isn't taking any chances—she's decorating eggs for her own Easter egg hunt! "Easter is very simple," Lucy explains to Linus. "You paint the eggs. You hide the eggs. You find the eggs. And you know who's going to find them? Me!"

As she and Linus hide the eggs, Lucy writes down where each egg is hidden so that they'll be easy to find. Lucy is going to have the best Easter egg hunt ever!

But when Easter morning dawns, the rest of the gang isn't quite as excited as Lucy. They've been up for hours with no sign of the Easter Beagle!

"Marcie, I'm really sorry," Peppermint Patty says, shaking her head. "It's Easter morning, and we don't have any colored eggs. I've seen this happen on holidays before: You look forward to being happy, and then something happens that spoils it all."

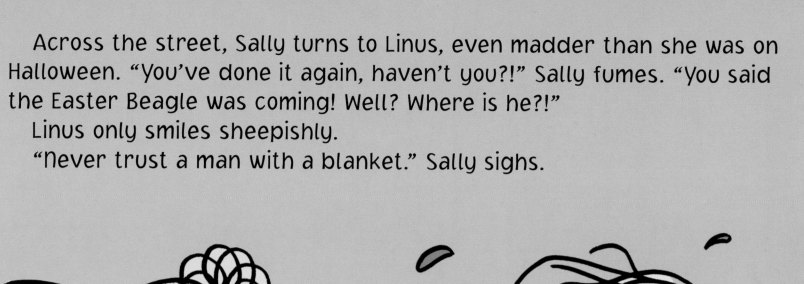

Across the street, Sally turns to Linus, even madder than she was on Halloween. "You've done it again, haven't you?!" Sally fumes. "You said the Easter Beagle was coming! Well? Where is he?!"

Linus only smiles sheepishly.

"Never trust a man with a blanket." Sally sighs.

Just when the gang thinks that Easter is ruined for sure, someone wonderful comes into view, dancing joyfully across the meadow!

"It's him!" Linus gasps. "The Easter Beagle is coming!"

The Easter Beagle dances through the flowers, over to Linus and Sally, Marcie and Peppermint Patty, Schroeder and Woodstock and Lucy, giving them each a beautifully decorated egg.

But when the Easter Beagle finally reaches Charlie Brown, he turns his basket over—it's empty! Poor Charlie Brown. There are no eggs left for him. Charlie Brown is disappointed, but he's used to it.

Marcie turns to Peppermint Patty. "What do we do with Easter eggs now that we have them, sir?"

"We put a little salt on them, and we eat them," Peppermint Patty says.

Marcie pulls out a saltshaker from her pocket and salts the egg, then she takes a big bite of it—shell and all! *CRUNCH!* "Tastes terrible, sir."

Peppermint Patty can't believe what she's seeing. Marcie will always be her friend, but she's not sure Marcie will ever understand Easter traditions.

Sally and Linus bring their eggs over to Lucy. "See? Linus was right!" Sally says, smiling. "There *is* an Easter Beagle!"

"Some Easter Beagle!" Lucy scoffs, examining the egg she got. It looks awfully familiar. "He gave me my own egg!"

Lucy had spent all day decorating and hiding her own eggs for nothing—the Easter Beagle had just scooped them up and given them away!

But Lucy isn't about to let the Easter Beagle get away with it. She storms right over to Snoopy's doghouse, ready for a fight. "Come on, beagle! Put up your dukes!"

But then Lucy gets the best Easter surprise of all: Snoopy climbs down from his doghouse and gives her a big Easter kiss! Lucy feels all her anger melt away—she's suddenly giddy with all the wonder of springtime.

"Oh, that Easter Beagle," Lucy says with a big smile.